Flora

the Fancy Dress Fairy

For Zoë Sarankin,
a very good friend of the fairies

Special thanks to
Narinder Dhami

www.rainbowmagic.co.uk

ORCHARD BOOKS
338 Euston Road, London NW1 3BH
Orchard Books Australia
Level 17/207 Kent Street, Sydney, NSW 2000
A Paperback Original

First published in 2007 by Orchard Books
Text © Working Partners Limited 2007
Rainbow Magic is a registered trademark of Working Partners Limited
Series created by Working Partners Limited, London W6 0QT
Cover illustrations © Georgie Ripper 2007
Inside illustrations © Orchard Books 2007

A CIP catalogue record for this book is available
from the British Library.

ISBN: 978 1 84616 505 4

1 3 5 7 9 10 8 6 4 2
Printed in Great Britain

Orchard Books is a division of Hachette Children's Books

www.orchardbooks.co.uk

Flora
the Fancy Dress Fairy

by Daisy Meadows

ORCHARD BOOKS

The Fairyland Palace

Battlements

Courtyard

Jack Frost's Flag

Bedroom

Castle Moat

The Great Cake Robbery

Contents

McKersey Castle

"Rachel, look!" Kirsty Tate cried excitedly, pointing through the car window. "There's McKersey Castle!"

Rachel Walker, Kirsty's best friend, stared down the long drive at the huge, greystone castle ahead. It was set on a hill, amid sweeping grounds, and it had two tall turrets, one on either side of the entrance gate.

"It's beautiful," Rachel breathed.

Mrs Tate, who was driving, smiled in agreement. "Isn't it the perfect place for a party?" she said. "It was so clever of Lindsay and Robert to choose a castle for their fancy dress ball."

Lindsay was Kirsty's cousin, and she and her husband were celebrating their tenth wedding anniversary at McKersey Castle. Kirsty and her parents had been invited, and Kirsty was allowed to bring a friend, so

Rachel had travelled with the Tates all the way to the Scottish Highlands.

"It's a *masked* ball too," Mr Tate added.

"That'll be fun," Rachel said eagerly.

Kirsty nodded. "Wow!" she exclaimed as they drew closer to the castle. "There's a moat and a drawbridge!"

"Just like a fairytale castle," Rachel said, smiling at Kirsty.

Kirsty grinned at her friend. She and Rachel knew a great deal about fairies, because they'd met them many times. The girls and the fairies were now the best of friends, and that was Rachel and Kirsty's very special and magical secret.

The two girls watched with delight as the car crossed the drawbridge and

came to a stop in the courtyard. "Look at the battlements." Rachel said, as she and Kirsty climbed out of the car.

"I wonder if we're allowed to go up there."

"Hello!" cried Lindsay, Kirsty's cousin, rushing out of the large oak doors with her husband Robert. She hugged the Tates one by one. "And you must be Rachel," Lindsay said, giving Rachel a hug too. "Come inside, everyone."

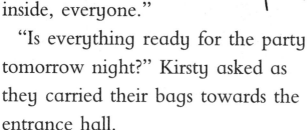

"Is everything ready for the party tomorrow night?" Kirsty asked as they carried their bags towards the entrance hall.

"Not quite!" Lindsay replied. "The cake is coming today, and the party planning company who are organising everything are delivering the fancy dress costumes tomorrow. You'll be able to choose your outfits then."

"The other guests are arriving tomorrow too," Robert added, as they stepped into the entrance hall.

Inside the castle, it was
cool and welcoming.
There were tall arched
windows, a flagstone
floor, and a suit of
armour standing
in one corner.
Colourful
embroidered
banners and
tapestries hung
from the ceiling
over the walls.
"I've picked out
a special bedroom for you
two," Lindsay said to Kirsty
and Rachel, as Robert led Mr and
Mrs Tate to their room. "Follow me."

Lindsay led the girls up a winding staircase. "Ta-dah!" she announced, throwing open a small wooden door.

Rachel and Kirsty gasped with delight when they saw the huge room with its two canopied beds and pretty white furniture. One side of the room was taken up with an enormous window,

and after the girls had put their bags down, they went to look out.

"We're right over the drawbridge!" Rachel cried excitedly.

"This used to be the old gatehouse," Lindsay explained.

"And where does that door by the wardrobe lead?" asked Kirsty.

"Come and see," Lindsay replied. The door opened onto another narrow staircase which led to the castle battlements. "Look!" Rachel said, pointing across the hills. "We're so high, it seems like we can see the whole of Scotland!"

"I gave you that bedroom because I thought you two girls would be great at protecting the castle from intruders," Lindsay joked, her eyes twinkling. "I don't want anything to spoil this party!"

Suddenly, Kirsty spotted a white van approaching the drawbridge. "'McKersey Village Cakes'," she read from the side of the van.

"My cake!" Lindsay cried, hurrying over to the stairs. "I'm dying to see it, girls! It was so difficult to arrange, but a party's no good without a cake, is it?"

She grinned at them. "Be careful up here, won't you?"

The girls nodded. "Lindsay's really excited, isn't she?" Kirsty laughed, as her cousin clattered off down the stairs.

"So am I!" Rachel said, smiling, but then she shivered. "Ooh! Did you just feel that blast of icy wind, Kirsty?"

"Yes," Kirsty agreed, frowning.

Rachel's eyes widened. "I can see ice!" she gasped, pointing. "There, all over the steps up to that turret!" The girls hurried over to investigate the turret to the left of the drawbridge.

Curiously they began to climb the frozen steps. As they did so, the air got colder and colder. And then, suddenly, Rachel and Kirsty heard a horribly familiar, icy voice.

"Raise my flag to the top of this tower!" it snapped.

Hardly daring to breathe, the two girls peeped round the turret up to the top of the steps. To their utter dismay, standing there, next to a gnarled green goblin, was Jack Frost himself!

Fairies to the Rescue

"Nothing will stop me holding my Icicle Party here tomorrow night," Jack Frost declared, as his goblin servant struggled with the flag. "Certainly not a pesky human fancy dress party!"

Rachel and Kirsty glanced at each other in horror. Jack Frost was planning a party at the castle on the same night as Lindsay and Robert!

"This is the perfect place for my party," Jack Frost continued. "It's miles from anywhere!"

At last the goblin managed to haul the flag to the top of the flagpole. As it unfurled, Rachel and Kirsty saw that it was a picture of Jack Frost wearing a golden crown.

"Now we have to get rid of the humans," Jack Frost mused. "We will return to my ice castle immediately, and plan how to ruin this silly fancy dress party before it's even begun!" And with a loud cackle, Jack Frost

zoomed away with the goblin on
a blast of icy wind.

"They've gone," Rachel said, relieved.

"But they'll be back!" Kirsty pointed
out. "And how are we going to
stop them ruining Lindsay and
Robert's party?"

Rachel thought for a moment. "We
could ask the fairies for help," she
suggested. "We have our lockets full of
fairy dust to take us to Fairyland."

Kirsty nodded eagerly.
"Maybe the Party
Fairies can help
us," she said,
as she and
Rachel opened
their lockets.

The girls sprinkled the glittering fairy
dust over their heads,
and immediately
found themselves
tumbling through
the air, shrinking
into fairies and
surrounded by
dancing rainbows.
As the rainbow colours
drifted away, Rachel and Kirsty floated
gently to the ground outside the pink
Fairyland palace.

"Shall we knock on the door?" Rachel
asked. It was the first time they'd ever
arrived in Fairyland without anyone to
meet them.

Kirsty nodded, so Rachel lifted the

butterfly-shaped door-knocker and
tapped on the door.

Almost straightaway, Bertram the frog
footman hopped out.
"Hello, girls!" he
exclaimed,
looking surprised.
"Welcome to
Fairyland once
again."

"Hello, Bertram," said
Kirsty, "Could we see the King and
Queen, please?"

Bertram bowed and took a small
silver bell off the table. He shook it.

"*Kirsty and Rachel to see the King
and Queen!*" sang out a silvery,
chiming voice.

The girls listened in amazement as inside the palace lots of bells tinkled, passing on the same message from room to room.

"The King and Queen will see you now!" a message came tinkling back.

"Follow me to the audience chamber, please," said Bertram.

The King and Queen were sitting on their glittering golden thrones when Bertram showed the girls into the chamber. It was a large room with a domed ceiling studded with silver stars.

"This is a pleasant surprise," said King Oberon. "Do you need our help, girls?" asked Queen Titania kindly.

"Your Majesty, Jack Frost is trying to spoil my cousin's party at McKersey Castle tomorrow," Kirsty explained.

"He wants to hold his own party there instead," added Rachel.

"We are holding our annual costume ball here at the palace tomorrow night," Queen Titania said, frowning.

"Maybe Jack Frost didn't receive his invitation, and that's why he's throwing his own party."

"Can you help us?" asked Kirsty.

"Yes, we know just the fairy to help," declared the King.

The Queen smiled and waved her wand, and a cascade of multi-coloured sparkles streamed out of the open window.

A few moments later, a fairy zoomed in and landed gently on the marble floor. Rachel and Kirsty stared at her.

The fairy was dressed as Snow White, in a long red dress, and carried a basket with an apple inside.

"This is Flora the Fancy Dress Fairy," said the Queen.

"Hi, girls!" Flora beamed at them. "How can I help you?"

The girls quickly explained about Jack Frost's nasty plans to ruin Richard and Lindsay's party. Flora shook her head, looking quite annoyed.

"Don't worry," she said firmly, "we won't let Jack Frost spoil the party!"

Goblin Trouble

"We can stop Jack Frost and those naughty goblins from ruining everything," Flora went on, "just as long as they don't get hold of my magic fancy dress items."

"What are they?" asked Kirsty.

"Flora's magic items change all the time," the Queen explained. "Just like

Flora's costumes!"
Flora nodded. "At
the moment, and for
Lindsay's party, my
three magic
items are a
porcelain figurine in
a princess gown,
a Red Riding Hood
cape and a black mask
with rainbow-coloured
feathers," she told the girls.
"The figurine will make the party food
wonderful, the cape helps the costumes
look good, and the mask ensures all the
guests have a great time."

"So if the goblins get hold of those
three magic things, they will be able

to spoil Lindsay's party?" asked
Kirsty nervously.

"Yes, but luckily Jack Frost and the
goblins don't know what they are!"
Flora laughed. "Now, let's hurry to
McKersey Castle and keep an eye on
the party preparations. Just let me
change my outfit."

Flora waved her wand over her head,
and a shower of turquoise and emerald
sparkles drifted down around her.

Rachel and Kirsty watched in
amazement as the fairy's long,
curly hair became a tumble of green
and blue ringlets,
topped with
a tiara of shells.
Flora's red dress
became a blue
bandana top
and, best of all,
a shimmering,
iridescent turquoise
skirt which curved
up into a beautiful
mermaid's tail at her ankles.

"What a gorgeous costume!" Kirsty
breathed.

"Now, be sure to watch out for any

goblin tricks!" said the King, as the Queen lifted her wand to shower them with fairy magic.

The girls and Flora nodded as they were swept up in a cloud of fairy dust. A moment later they found themselves back on the battlements of McKersey Castle and Rachel and Kirsty were human-sized again.

Flora looked up at Jack Frost's flag and tutted. Then she waved her wand and immediately a stream of blue and green sparkles surrounded the flag. When they cleared, the picture of Jack Frost had vanished and an L and an R were intertwined in curly pink letters.

"That's better!" Flora declared.

Rachel was looking over the battlements at the courtyard below. The cake van was parked there, its back doors open. But the next second she spotted something else: goblins!

"There's a group of goblins around the cake van!" Rachel cried.

"The delivery man must be inside the castle with Lindsay," said Kirsty. "I hope he's taken the cake with him."

But as the girls and Flora watched, they saw three goblins climbing out of the van. They were holding a large cardboard box which they began to tear apart, revealing a beautiful three-tiered cake.

"The goblins have got Lindsay's cake!" Kirsty wailed.

"And, look," Rachel added, pointing at another smaller van, parked in the courtyard, with 'Jack Frost's Frosted Delights' written on the side. "They're going to drive away with it!"

Cake Chaos

"We'll get down there more quickly if you're fairy-sized, girls!" Flora said firmly, and, with a swish of her wand and a sparkle of magic, Rachel and Kirsty were fairies again. Immediately, the three friends flew over the battlements and zoomed down to the courtyard.

"Oh, no!" Flora exclaimed as they hovered above the goblins. "My magic figurine is on top of the cake!"

Rachel and Kirsty looked closer. On top of the white and silver icing was a delicate porcelain figure wearing a gorgeous, flowing, yellow dress.

"So if the goblins steal it, then *all* the party food will be spoilt?" Rachel asked in dismay.

Flora nodded, whizzing down to confront the goblins, with Kirsty and Rachel close behind.

"Put the cake down!" Flora
demanded.

One of the goblins poked his tongue
out. "Go away, pesky
fairies!" he jeered.
"We're taking this
cake to Jack Frost
for his party."

Another goblin
grabbed a chunk of
icing from the cake and
flung it at Flora and the girls, so
that they had to dodge quickly out
of the way.

The other goblins cackled with glee
and immediately started pulling off
chunks of cake and hurling them in the
direction of Flora, Rachel and Kirsty.

"Help!" Rachel cried, as a large piece almost hit her.

"They're ruining the cake!" Kirsty gasped.

Frowning, Flora lifted her wand. Suddenly a *whoosh* of magic sparkles sent a piece of the cake zooming back towards the goblin who'd thrown it. It hit him in the mouth and he recoiled. Then he licked his lips.

"Yum!" he declared. He pulled off another lump of cake, but this time, instead of hurling it at the girls, he ate it.

"Greedy-guts!" hollered the goblin next to him, but he stuffed a bit of cake into his mouth too.

"Leave some for us!" the other goblins shouted, and they also began gobbling chunks of cake.

"Stop!" the biggest goblin shouted suddenly. "Jack Frost's waiting for us. We'd better put the cake in the van."

As the goblins struggled to load the enormous cake into the back of their van, Flora, Rachel and Kirsty wondered what they could do to stop them.

JACK FROST'S FROSTED DELIGHTS

"Oh!" Rachel gasped suddenly. "They'll have to drive over the drawbridge to get out, won't they?"

Kirsty nodded. Then she grinned, catching on. "So if we lift the drawbridge up, they won't be able to leave!" she cried. "That's brilliant, Rachel!"

The goblins had piled into the van and were already on their way. Quickly, Flora waved her wand and pointed it at the drawbridge.

Instantly, emerald sparks zipped towards the heavy chains which raised and lowered the bridge, and, very slowly, the drawbridge began to rise.

"Look at the drawbridge!" squawked one of the goblins. "Go faster! We have to get out!"

The biggest goblin put his foot down and the van shot forwards.

"It's no good!" Rachel cried. "The drawbridge isn't lifting fast enough!"

A Piece of Cake

As the van careered towards the rising
drawbridge, Flora flicked her wrist,
sending more fairy magic streaming
through the air. Rachel and Kirsty held
their breath. Just as the goblins reached
the drawbridge, it swung swiftly
upwards and slammed closed, trapping
the goblins' van inside the castle.

"Thanks, Flora," Kirsty said.
Flora winked at her,
then waved her wand
again and turned
Rachel and Kirsty
back to their
human size. They
all hurried over to
the van.

"Now, give my
cousin's cake back," Kirsty said firmly.
"Or Flora will send you all to the
castle dungeons!"

The goblin in the driver's
seat looked sulky. He
muttered something
under his breath,
and, next moment,

the back doors of the van swung open. The goblins pushed the cake out onto the flagstones. *Splat!*

Kirsty and Rachel looked at each other in dismay. The tiers of the cake had collapsed, and the beautiful cake was completely ruined!

"Well, at least the magic figurine isn't broken," Kirsty said, picking it up carefully. "But everything else is!"

"Now let us out of here!" the goblin driver yelled crossly.

Flora waved her wand again, and, with a creak, the drawbridge slowly lowered. The goblins immediately

sped away. "Don't worry, girls, now I've got the figurine back, I can fix it," Flora said comfortingly. Then she grinned. "In fact, it will be a *piece of cake!*"

As she spoke, she sent a swirl of fairy magic in the direction of the ruined cake on the floor. The mess vanished in an instant, and, in the twinkling of an eye, a beautiful, glittering five-tiered cake appeared, with little arches holding up each layer. White and pink iced flowers tumbled down the sides of the cake, and, as well as the magic figurine on top, small figures in fancy dress danced in between the different layers.

"Oh!" Kirsty breathed, "It's the most amazing cake I've ever seen!"

Rachel nodded in agreement as a cardboard box magically appeared and folded itself around the cake.

Just then, Lindsay and the delivery man came out into the courtyard. Flora darted into Kirsty's pocket.

Looking excited, Lindsay opened the cake box. "Oh!" she exclaimed in awe. "What a *beautiful* cake! It's turned out even better than I imagined!"

"It *is* lovely, isn't it?" Rachel said with a grin.

"Magical!" Lindsay sighed, and the girls exchanged a secret smile.

"You know, I was worried because everything in the kitchens just now has been awful!" Lindsay went on. "The chefs were getting all the recipes wrong, and the ovens weren't working properly. But this fabulous cake has made me feel a lot better!" She turned to the delivery man. "Could you help me carry it inside, please?"

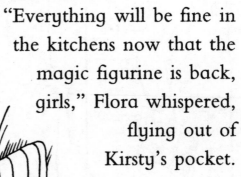

"Everything will be fine in the kitchens now that the magic figurine is back, girls," Flora whispered, flying out of Kirsty's pocket.

"Thank goodness," Rachel said.

"I must return to Fairyland," Flora went on, "but I'll be back – and so will Jack Frost's goblins, so be on your guard! And, with that, she blew the girls a kiss and vanished.

Rachel and Kirsty smiled at each other, looking determined. They'd saved Flora's magic figurine and so the party food wouldn't be ruined, but what tricks would Jack Frost's goblins try next?

The Big Costume Kidnap

Contents

Colourful Costumes

"Jack Frost must be annoyed that his goblins didn't get away with the cake!" Rachel said to Kirsty with a smile.

It was the following morning and the girls were walking downstairs into the entrance hall of the castle. Sunshine was streaming in through the arched windows, and everyone else was bustling here and there, busy with final preparations for the party that evening.

"Yes, so we *must* keep a look-out for more goblin mischief today," Kirsty replied, as Lindsay hurried by, carrying a vase of flowers. "We haven't got to get ready for the party for ages yet, so shall we ask Lindsay if there's anything we can do?"

"Good idea," Rachel agreed.

The two girls went over to Lindsay.

"Can we help?" asked Kirsty.

"Oh, thank you!" Lindsay said
gratefully, placing the
flowers on a table.
"The costumes
arrived an hour
ago and they've
been put in one
of the bedrooms.
Do you think you
could check them
and make sure that
all the outfits have the
right accessories with them?"

The girls nodded, so Lindsay led them
quickly towards one of the bedrooms on
the second floor.

"Most of the guests will be arriving in

the next couple of hours," Lindsay explained. "So they'll be coming to choose their costumes then, but you two can have first pick." She stopped outside a heavy wooden door. "They're all in here."

"*Hee hee hee!*" Kirsty jumped as she heard a nasty little muffled giggle coming from inside the room. Unfortunately, she knew exactly who giggled like that: goblins! She glanced at Rachel and Lindsay. Kirsty could tell from Rachel's face that she'd heard it too, but luckily Lindsay hadn't noticed so far.

"So," Rachel said quickly, stepping in front of Lindsay so that she didn't open the door, "you want us to check that all the costumes are displayed properly?"

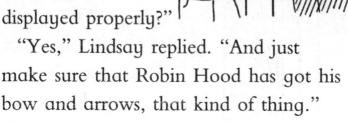

"Yes," Lindsay replied. "And just make sure that Robin Hood has got his bow and arrows, that kind of thing."

"We'll be fine, Lindsay," Kirsty told her. "You can leave us to it. You must have lots to do!"

"Oh, yes," Lindsay agreed. "I must
check on the decorations in
the ballroom. Thank
you, girls." And she
hurried off.

"Watch out for
goblins!" Kirsty
told Rachel
as she opened
the door.

Rachel
groaned as the
door swung
inward to reveal
two giggling
goblins pulling
costumes off the racks!

The room was a complete mess.

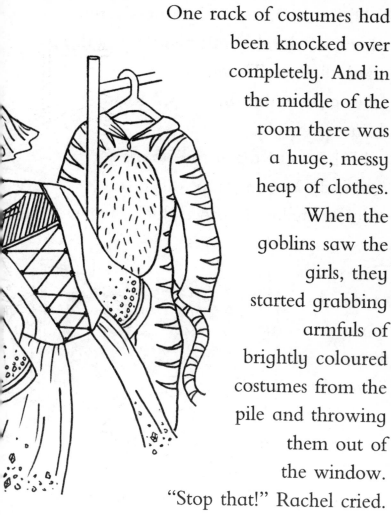

One rack of costumes had been knocked over completely. And in the middle of the room there was a huge, messy heap of clothes. When the goblins saw the girls, they started grabbing armfuls of brightly coloured costumes from the pile and throwing them out of the window.

"Stop that!" Rachel cried.

The goblins each seized another armful of clothes and then they both climbed onto the windowsill.

"They're going to jump!" Kirsty shouted.

As she and Rachel ran across the room, the goblins leapt out of the window, holding onto a thick, heavy

rope. The girls saw that the rope had been tied to one of the wardrobes in the room. The other end dangled out of the window. The goblins were making their escape by lowering themselves down the castle wall, holding onto the rope.

"Look!" Kirsty cried, pointing down at the moat.

A rowing-boat was bobbing gently in the water. Three more goblins sat in the boat, surrounded by all the stolen costumes, hats and shoes that the two goblins had thrown out of the window.

Kirsty's heart sank as she spotted a bright red hooded cape on top of the pile. It was shimmering slightly with fairy magic.

"Oh, no!" she gasped. "They've got Flora's magic Red Riding Hood cape!"

Boat on the
Moat

"Let's get down there!" Kirsty replied,
running for the door with Rachel at her
heels. "What a shame Flora isn't here to
turn us into fairies!"

The girls dashed down the stairs and
into the entrance hall, which was now
empty. Suddenly the visor in the suit of
armour in the corner snapped open.

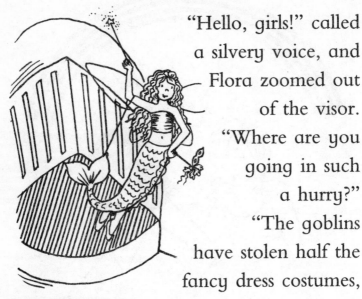

"Hello, girls!" called a silvery voice, and Flora zoomed out of the visor. "Where are you going in such a hurry?"

"The goblins have stolen half the fancy dress costumes, including your magic cape!" Rachel explained. "And they've got a boat to escape across the moat!"

"We've got to stop them!" Flora exclaimed.

She and the girls raced out of the hall, through the courtyard and onto the drawbridge.

"There they are!" Kirsty yelled,
pointing.

The goblins were rowing furiously
away from the drawbridge towards the
bend in the moat. As they disappeared

around the side of the castle, Rachel
turned to Flora. "We must stop them
getting away!" she cried.

But Flora shook her head. "Don't worry, girls," she replied calmly. "Just wait here."

Puzzled, Rachel and Kirsty glanced at each other. The goblins were escaping with the magic cape, and Flora didn't seem worried at all!

A moment later, Rachel and Kirsty heard the splashing of oars behind them. The girls spun round to see the silly goblins rowing towards them from around the other side of the castle. "The goblins have gone round in a circle!" Kirsty laughed. "They can't have realised that the moat surrounds the castle."

Rachel and Flora grinned.

"Hey!" one of the goblins screeched suddenly. "There's the drawbridge. We're back where we started!"

"This is all your fault!" yelled another goblin, glaring at the two who were rowing the boat.

"I'm going to throw you into the moat, and the alligators will eat you!"

"I'm not scared of alligators!" shouted one of the rowers. Then he paused. "Er, what's an alligator anyway?"

"I know what an alligator is," said one of the other goblins importantly. "It's pink and it has eight legs!"

"No, that's not an alligator," the first goblin yelled crossly. "That's an elephant!"

The goblins began to push and poke each other as they argued. The two who

were rowing dropped their oars and joined in, and the boat began to drift aimlessly towards the drawbridge.

"Maybe we can lean over and grab the magic cape," Rachel whispered, as the boat approached.

"Especially as the goblins are arguing too much to take any notice of us," added Kirsty.

"Good idea." Flora nodded. "Let's go for it!"

Goblins get Dressed

Rachel and Kirsty lay down on the drawbridge and dangled their arms over the moat as the boat drew nearer. But just as Rachel reached out her hand to snatch the sparkling red cape, one of the goblins looked up and spotted them.

"They're trying to steal our costumes!" he yelled, grabbing one of the oars.

"Get away from the drawbridge! Row for the bank!"

Rachel, Kirsty and Flora watched in dismay as the goblins rowed away as fast as they could.

"I nearly got the cape, too," Rachel groaned, scrambling to her feet.

The goblins had reached the bank now and were throwing the costumes out of the boat onto the grass. Then they jumped out of the boat themselves. As Rachel, Kirsty and Flora rushed

across the
drawbridge
towards the
boat, they
heard the
goblins yelling
at each other.
"There are too
many costumes for us to carry!" one
shouted. "What shall we do?"

"Put some of the clothes on!"
screeched another goblin,
struggling to get into
a pair of red velvet
breeches. He popped
a white curly wig on
his head, and then
a sailor's hat on top.

"We can carry the rest!"
    As Flora and the girls
hurried towards the
bank, they watched
in amazement as
the goblins
dressed
themselves up.
One put on
a tiger outfit
with a tail,
and then
a sparkly
waistcoat,
a clown's red nose,
and three hats,
including a straw one with
a plastic flower on it. Another was

wearing a pink clown wig with a golden crown on top. He also had the magic cape slung round his neck, but the hood kept falling forwards over his face; because the costumes were human-sized, they were much too big for the goblins. All of them were wearing odd shoes which didn't fit, and they kept tripping over as they rushed around scooping up the rest of the outfits.

Flora, Rachel and Kirsty couldn't help laughing as they reached the bank.

"Hand over those costumes!" Flora called in her silvery voice.

"No!" shouted the goblin with the cape. "Jack Frost's holding his party

here tonight, so you won't be
needing these!"

His friends cackled gleefully. Then one
of them picked up a long princess gown
and threw it right over Rachel and
Kirsty's heads, trapping Flora, too, who
was fluttering alongside the girls.

"Help!" Rachel cried.

"Everything's gone dark!" Kirsty gasped.

Goblins Meet Goats

As the girls and Flora struggled
to free themselves from the heavy
dress, they heard the goblins
rushing away, chuckling.

"We have to catch them!" Rachel
panted as she and Kirsty finally
managed to throw off the dress.

"Look, they've left some of the

costumes behind," said
Kirsty, pointing at
a heap of clothes
on the bank.

Rachel looked
worried. "We can't
leave them here in case Lindsay finds
them," she said, picking up an
embroidered jacket. "But we can't
carry them while we run after the
goblins either."

Kirsty frowned as she looked
more closely at the jacket
Rachel was holding.
"The sleeves are
almost falling off!"
she exclaimed,
pointing at the jacket.

96

"Look, the stitches are loose."

"That's because the magic cape is missing," Flora explained. "The costumes are starting to fall apart at the seams!"

"Oh, no!" Rachel sighed. "The party will be ruined if we don't get the cape back."

Kirsty turned to Flora.

"Flora, could you shrink the costumes?" she suggested eagerly. "Then they'd fit into our pockets!"

"Sure!" Flora laughed, waving her wand.

A swirl of fairy dust later, and a neat pile of tiny clothes, shoes and hats lay on the bank. Rachel and Kirsty knelt down and carefully filled their pockets.

Then they raced off after the goblins.

The goblins had set off across the moors. Luckily Flora and the girls could see the magic cape shimmering ahead of them in the distance, so they could easily keep track of where the goblins were going.

"Look, there's a cowboy hat," Rachel panted, seeing the hat lying on the grass.

"And there's a pink clown wig," Kirsty added, pointing a little further ahead. "The goblins must have dropped them."

Quickly, Flora shrunk the hat and the wig and the girls popped them into their pockets. Then they hurried after the goblins, picking up other fancy dress items that the goblins had dropped along the way.

A bit further on, Kirsty stopped and shaded her eyes, peering ahead to see

 where the goblins were. She saw them climbing a steep slope, heading up a mountain, towards a herd of mountain goats. That gave Kirsty an idea.

"Somehow we have to get the goblins to stop so that we can catch up!" Kirsty said urgently to Flora. "Do you think your magic could ask those goats to help us?"

"What a great idea!" Flora beamed. She pointed her wand at the goats and a stream of green and blue bubbles floated through the air towards the herd. The bubbles drifted towards the goats' ears and then burst gently, making little bleating sounds.

"*Baa! Baa!*"

"That's goat language," Flora explained, as Rachel and Kirsty smiled.

The goats looked up from the grass. Then, as Flora and the girls watched, all the goats trotted over to stand in front of the goblins, blocking their path.

The goblins skidded to a halt and stared nervously at the hairy creatures.

Flora, Rachel and Kirsty hurried to
catch up. As they got closer, they could
see the goblins shaking with fear.

"Are these alligators?" asked one
fearfully.

"No," said the one with the cape.
"I think they might be Pogwurzels!"

"*Pogwurzels?*" chorused the others in alarm.

"Yes. And we all know that Pogwurzels eat goblins!" the one with the cape wailed.

All the goblins shrieked with terror as one of the goats trotted forward. It leaned over to sniff the plastic flower on the straw hat. "Please don't eat me, Mr Pogwurzel!" the goblin wearing the hat begged, too petrified to move.

104

"He looks hungry!" Rachel called,
although she was secretly quite sure that
goats didn't eat goblins.

"Maybe they want to eat the clothes,"
shouted Kirsty, as another goat sniffed
at a goblin's sleeve.

Immediately, all the goblins threw
down the clothes
they were
carrying. The
goats sniffed
curiously
at the
costumes
but then
turned their
attention back
to the goblins.

With shrieks of fear, the goblins quickly pulled off all the items they were wearing.

The one with the magic cape took that off last of all. "Don't gobble me up, Mr Pogwurzel!" he begged, holding the cape out towards one of the goats. "This cloak is much tastier than I am."

The goat snorted, which was too much for the goblin. He squealed with fright, threw the cape on the ground and fled, his goblin friends charging after him.

Costume Clear-up

Flora, Rachel and Kirsty laughed.

"The goats won't really eat the costumes, will they?" Kirsty asked anxiously as the goats sniffed at the pile of costumes.

Flora shook her head as she shrank all the costumes, including the magic cape, so that the girls could gather them up and put them in their pockets. "Goats like young thistle plants best of all," she said. And with another wave of her

wand, she turned a large patch of purple heather into a field of thistles. The goats immediately bent their heads, took a sniff and began to gobble the thistles up.

"Thank you, goats!" called Flora and the girls as they set off back to McKersey Castle.

"Weren't the goblins silly?" Rachel laughed as they hurried back across the drawbridge.

Kirsty nodded. "And they did look funny wearing all those costumes," she added.

Soon they were back in the room where the fancy dress costumes were stored. The girls looked dismayed as they glanced around.

"I'd forgotten how much mess the goblins had made!" Kirsty sighed, staring at the overturned rack and the costumes strewn about. "How will we ever get this cleared up before Lindsay comes back?"

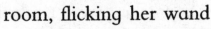

"No problem!" Flora announced cheerfully. "Leave this to me."

The little fairy danced around the room, flicking her wand here and there and sending little puffs of magical fairy dust whirling down onto the costumes. Rachel and Kirsty watched in delight as the clothes lifted themselves up off the floor and floated in the air. Then they danced over to the racks, sleeves waving. The hats and wigs bobbed through the

air too, and all the shoes began to tap dance their way over to join their costumes.

"Look!" Rachel said to Kirsty. "All the clothes, hats and shoes are sorting themselves into the right outfits!"

Kirsty nodded as the curly pink wig bobbed past to join the red nose, stripy trousers and enormous shoes of the clown costume.

Then the tiny clothes began floating out of the girls' pockets.

As they danced through the air, the costumes grew back to their normal sizes before finding their places on the racks. And Rachel noticed that, with the magic cape safe and sound, the sleeves on the embroidered jacket weren't loose any more.

"This is brilliant, Flora!" Kirsty exclaimed as the last few pieces of the costumes moved into place. "Look at this, Rachel. All the men's costumes are, *here* and the ladies' costumes are on this rack *here*." "And the animal costumes are on a separate rack," Rachel

added, pointing at the tiger costume
and others. "Thank you so much, Flora.
All the costumes look perfect!"

Flora beamed at them. "You've got
one item left in your pocket,
Kirsty," she said.
And, as she spoke,
the magic red
cape floated out.

"I want
someone special
to wear it," Flora
said thoughtfully.
"Let me see... Aha!"
Her face lit up and she lifted her wand.
Immediately, the Red Riding Hood dress
and basket lifted themselves off the rack
and floated over to settle on a chair.

The magic cape drifted over to join them, growing back to its normal size as it did so. Last of all, a big white label appeared in a burst of magic sparkles and pinned itself to the cape.

"'Mrs Tate'," Kirsty read aloud. "Rachel, that costume's for my mum!"

With a gleam in her eyes, Flora tapped her wand on the chair. A furry grey wolf costume instantly appeared, with a label saying 'Mr Tate'. Kirsty and Rachel burst out laughing.

"That's fantastic, Flora!" Kirsty said gratefully. "Thank you."

"And thank *you*, girls," Flora said with a wide smile. "But don't forget that Jack Frost will still be doing his very best to stop the party from going ahead. Or, should I say, his very *worst*!"

Kirsty and Rachel nodded.

"We'll be careful," Rachel promised.

"Now I must go back to Fairyland, and you two had better choose yourself some fancy dress costumes," Flora said with a wink. "I'm sure that you'll find the *perfect* costumes if you look hard enough!"

And as Rachel and Kirsty waved, the little fairy disappeared in a colourful swirl of glittering fairy magic.

The Magic
Mask Mystery

Contents

Lindsay's Angels

"Hello, girls!" The door opened and Lindsay came in. "Wow! You've done a *great* job!" she declared, looking around.

Rachel and Kirsty smiled. Flora's magic had finished tidying the room just in time.

"And have you chosen your outfits?" Lindsay asked.

Rachel and Kirsty glanced at each other excitedly. Flora had said that she was sure they'd find the perfect fancy dress costumes. Had she worked some fairy magic and left special outfits just for them?

Kirsty's face lit up as she suddenly noticed a few blue and green sparkles floating around one of the racks. "Actually, we were just about to have a look," she said, nudging Rachel.

Rachel spotted the sparkles too, and together the two girls hurried over to the rack. There, hanging at one end, they found two beautiful angel costumes. The dainty white dresses sparkled with a silver sheen and there were matching feathery wings, delicate haloes and silver cardboard angel harps. White feather masks glittering with silver sparkles completed the outfits.

Rachel and Kirsty looked at each other in delight as they took the gorgeous costumes off the rack. "We'd *love* to wear these outfits," Kirsty said to Lindsay. "Well, I don't even remember seeing *those*," Lindsay said with a smile, "but they *are* lovely and they'll suit you both perfectly!"

They all turned round as the door opened again and Mr and Mrs Tate came in, followed by several couples.

"All the guests have arrived now, so we're bringing them to choose their costumes," Mrs Tate explained.

Lindsay smiled at everyone. "Why don't you go and change?" she said to the girls. "Then go and have a peep at the ballroom decorations."

Rachel and Kirsty nodded happily.

"Mum, Dad," Kirsty called as she headed for the door with her angel outfit. "Your costumes are on the chair."

Mr and Mrs Tate laughed in delight when they saw the Red Riding Hood and wolf costumes. Laughing too, Rachel and Kirsty hurried off to their room.

"I'll help you put up your hair, and then you can help me with mine," Rachel said as they slipped the pretty white dresses on. "Then we can fix the haloes on top."

Soon the girls were ready.

"Don't our costumes look fantastic?" Rachel said as they stood side by side admiring themselves in the mirror.

"Yes, thanks to Flora," Kirsty
agreed happily.

"Let's go downstairs and look at
the ballroom," suggested Rachel.
"The party will be starting soon,
and I can't wait!"

Carrying their harps, the girls went
downstairs to the enormous ballroom.
The doors stood open and Rachel and
Kirsty peeped inside.
The room was
empty as all
the other
guests were
still dressing.

"Isn't it
beautiful?"
Kirsty breathed.

The ballroom was decorated in white and gold. There were long white curtains, held back by twisted golden ropes at the windows, glittering crystal chandeliers hanging from the ceiling, and sprays of white roses on all the tables. There were also white marble statues wearing beautiful fancy dress masks placed around the room.

"I don't think any of these masks are

Flora's magic one," remarked Rachel.
"Don't forget that we have to make
sure the goblins don't get hold of it,
Kirsty, or the party will be ruined!"

Kirsty nodded. "There's the cake,"
she said, pointing to a table at the
other end of the room. The girls went
to have a closer look and placed their
harps on the table.

"It looks even more beautiful here in the ballroom," Rachel said admiringly. But Kirsty was distracted by a blue and emerald figurine on the cake's middle tier. "Look!" she exclaimed. "That figure looks just like Flora!"

"Yes, it does," Rachel agreed.

Suddenly the figurine winked at them! Rachel and Kirsty were so startled, they almost dropped their harps. "It *is* Flora!" Kirsty laughed. "Hello," called Flora, zipping over to the girls with a big smile.

Before Rachel could reply,
a movement out in the courtyard
caught her eye. She glanced out of the
window and saw a group of rather
odd-looking guests. They were very
short and had extremely large feet.
"Goblins!" Rachel gasped in
dismay. "They're arriving for
Jack Frost's party!"

Goblin Guests

"We must stop them!" Flora said firmly, and the three friends rushed out of the ballroom.

There were five goblins outside, all dressed in top hats and tails. They were heading towards the entrance hall door as Flora, Rachel and Kirsty emerged into the courtyard.

"Hello!" Rachel called quickly, "Are you coming to Lindsay and Robert's party?"

"No!" snapped one of the goblins. "We're going to *Jack Frost's* party!"

"Oh, that's not *here*," Kirsty put in. "I expect it will be at his ice castle."

Muttering grumpily, the goblin pulled out a large invitation card. "It says here that Jack Frost's party is taking place at *McKersey Castle!*" he said loudly.

The girls glanced nervously at Flora. The little fairy grinned and aimed her wand at the invitation. A few magic sparkles went zooming towards it.

"Tell him to check again!" she whispered to Kirsty.

"Are you sure you haven't made a mistake?" Kirsty asked the goblin.

"Of course!" the goblin said rudely, shoving the invitation under the girls' noses. "It says—" But then he stopped, his eyes almost 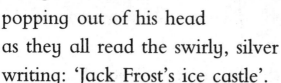 popping out of his head as they all read the swirly, silver writing: 'Jack Frost's ice castle'.

"The party *is* at Jack Frost's ice castle!" the goblin mumbled sheepishly.

The other goblins looked confused.

Muttering angrily, they all turned round and slunk away. "And tell your friends," Kirsty called after them, "that Jack Frost won't be happy if his guests are late!"

"Good!" Flora said with satisfaction, hiding on Kirsty's shoulder as the girls went inside. "That will keep some of the goblin guests away."

Inside the entrance hall people were gathering for the start of the party. Rachel and Kirsty smiled to see a man dressed as a scarecrow. He was standing rigidly in the corner with his arms stuck out.

"He's acting just like a *real* scarecrow!" Rachel whispered to Kirsty. "Isn't that funny?"

Kirsty nodded as a man in a cowboy outfit strolled towards them. "Howdy, girls," he said in an American accent, tipping his hat.

Rachel and Kirsty couldn't help laughing.

"*Grrr!*"

Startled by the sound of growling, the girls looked round. A woman dressed in the tiger outfit was staring at them. Then she sprang forward and Rachel and Kirsty had to jump out of the way.

"She's taking her costume a bit seriously!" Rachel whispered as the tiger woman began sharpening her claws.

Just then Lindsay rushed into
the entrance hall.
She wasn't wearing
her costume
and she looked
very upset.

"What's
the matter,
Lindsay?" asked
Kirsty anxiously.

"My mask is
missing!" Lindsay said, "and
I don't know where it's gone. It's
a complete mystery! It's black with
rainbow-coloured feathers. Have you
seen it?"

Rachel and Kirsty shook their heads,
glancing at each other in dismay.

They recognised the description: it was the magic mask!

"The goblins must have stolen my mask," Flora whispered, as Lindsay hurried round the entrance hall, asking the other guests.

"Is that why the guests are behaving so strangely?" Kirsty asked.

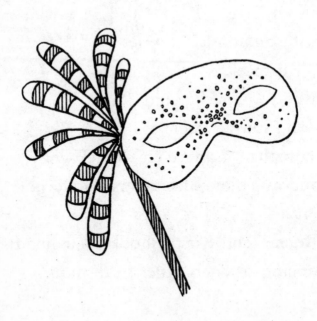

Flora nodded. "Yes," she said anxiously. "The fairy magic in your lockets must be protecting you two, but I think the other guests are *becoming* their fancy dress characters !"

Missing Mask

"Oh, no!" Rachel whispered. "Remember all those crazy costumes we sorted out? We have to find the magic mask or this party will be chaos!"

"Lindsay, we'll help you look," Kirsty called to her cousin. "Where did you last have your mask?"

Lindsay frowned. "I had it in the

ballroom," she said slowly, "and I had it in the wine cellar when I went to get a bottle of champagne."

"We'll look in the cellar while you search the ballroom," Rachel suggested.

Lindsay nodded. "Thanks, girls."

The entrance to the wine cellar wasn't far from the entrance hall.

Rachel and Kirsty climbed down the staircase into the stone cellar and began to look around. "What's that?" Kirsty asked, pointing at the flagstones.

There was a fine layer of dust on the floor and the girls and Flora could see footprints. Next to them lay a tiny pink feather.

"That's a feather from the magic mask!" Flora exclaimed. "And those are goblin footprints. Let's follow them."

The footprints led to a wall at the back of the cellar, where they stopped abruptly.

"Did the goblins use Jack Frost's magic to walk through the wall?" Kirsty wondered.

The girls peered closely at the wall and moved their hands over it carefully.

"I can feel a draught of air here!" Rachel said excitedly, with her hand on the join between two stones.

"A secret door!" Flora exclaimed.

Just then Rachel noticed a smooth, round indentation in one of the stones. She pressed it and immediately the wall swung back slowly. Rachel, Kirsty and

 Flora stared at the dark passageway that stretched away behind the wall.

"The goblins must have escaped down this secret passage with the mask," Kirsty said.

148

"Yes, I wonder where it goes," Rachel replied. "It's too dark to see." She looked nervous. "Jack Frost and his goblins might be hiding in there!"

Immediately Flora swished her wand lightly back and forth, and the tip began to glow with a bright light. Now Rachel and Kirsty could see into the passage ahead.

The three friends crept down the narrow corridor until they found themselves face to face with another stone wall.

"Oh!" Rachel said, disappointedly. "It's a dead end."

"Maybe not," Kirsty replied. She ran her hands over the stones and found a round indentation the same as the one that had opened the other wall. Kirsty pressed it and the wall began to move.

"Don't open it all the way, Kirsty," Flora hissed. "We don't know what's on the other side!"

Quickly, Kirsty took her finger off the indentation, so that the wall stayed open just a crack.

The girls and Flora peered through the narrow opening. Behind it was not a passageway, but they could see a cave-like room instead. They could also hear a familiar voice...

"Now, listen to me, goblins!" it was saying. "I'm going to tell you *exactly* how to ruin this pesky party!"

"Oh, no!" Kirsty whispered. "It's Jack Frost!"

Jack Frost Unmasked!

"I want you to steal every mask in the castle!" Jack Frost declared gleefully, sitting in a big chair before his goblins, his back to the girls. "And you must cause as much trouble as you can, while you're doing it. We have to get rid of these annoying humans!"

"Look at the mask in Jack Frost's

hand," Rachel whispered.

Kirsty and Flora stared at the mask. It was black with rainbow-coloured, plumy feathers, and it shimmered slightly with magic.

"It's my magic mask," Flora said softly.

"I'm going to wear *this* mask because it's the best one, and I'm the most important person!"

Jack Frost said boastfully, waving it in the air.

"He doesn't realise it's the magic mask," Flora said to Rachel and Kirsty.

"But how are we going to get it away from him?" Rachel asked.

"He's very close," Kirsty pointed out. "Maybe I can just grab the mask and we can make a run for it?"

"Let's try it," Flora agreed. "Once we have the mask, I'll use my magic to block the entrance to the secret passage so that you can escape."

Kirsty nodded, feeling extremely nervous as she edged her way carefully through the gap. She hoped that the goblins wouldn't spot her. Luckily, she was hidden by Jack Frost's chair.

"Now go and make sure every human in this castle is gone as soon as possible!" Jack Frost shouted at his goblins, waving the mask about again.

At that moment, Kirsty leaned forward and snatched the mask right out of Jack Frost's hand.

Jack Frost whipped round. "Stop that girl!" he roared, and all the goblins surged forward as Kirsty darted back into the passageway.

Rachel pulled the door closed behind Kirsty just as Jack Frost lifted his wand.

"This will stop them," said Flora, and she sent a whoosh of magical fairy dust towards the wall. The sparkles framed the door with a glittering outline, sealing it firmly shut.

Then Rachel, Kirsty and Flora dashed off down the secret passage.

A few moments later they were back in the entrance hall.

"That was close!" Rachel exclaimed. "I'm sure Jack Frost was about to cast a horrible spell!"

"You did brilliantly, Kirsty," Flora put in. "Now let's get the magic mask back to Lindsay as quickly as we can."

"There are Lindsay and Robert," Kirsty murmured. "Don't they look great?"

Rachel nodded.

"They look like the King and Queen of the Ball," she said with a smile.

Lindsay was dressed in a beautiful Tudor ballgown, with hooped skirts sewn with beads and sparkling jewels. Robert was wearing an embroidered jacket, knee breeches, and a stiff white ruff around his neck. They both wore gold crowns.

"Lindsay!" Kirsty called. "We found your mask." Lindsay stared down her nose at the girls. "How dare you approach me in such a rude manner?" she snapped haughtily. "Be gone, immediately!" Rachel and Kirsty stared at each other in confusion. "It's OK," Flora whispered from Kirsty's shoulder.

"Lindsay's just acting like a real queen because the mask isn't back in its proper place yet."

Quickly, Kirsty pressed the magic mask into Lindsay's hand. Immediately, Lindsay blinked a couple of times and then seemed to wake up, almost as though she'd been in a trance.

Robert and all the other guests did the same.

"Thank you, girls," Lindsay said gratefully, as Rachel and Kirsty glanced at each other in relief.

"Now we can start the party!" Kirsty said with a smile.

Fancy Dress in Fairyland

Lindsay and Robert led the guests to the ballroom, but Rachel and Kirsty hung back until the entrance hall was empty.

"Jack Frost and his goblins will leave now that the magic mask is back in its rightful place," Flora told the girls. "It will make sure the party goes smoothly.

So you will have nothing more to worry about."

"Thank you, Flora," Kirsty said gratefully. "Lindsay and Robert's party will be great now, thanks to you!"

"We did it together, girls!" Flora declared happily.

Suddenly, there was a flash of coloured light and a magical rainbow

streamed into the entrance hall. Rachel and Kirsty grinned as Bertram, the frog footman, hopped off the end of it.

"Good evening!" Bertram said, bowing low. "The King and Queen of Fairyland would like to invite Kirsty and Rachel to drop in on their fancy dress party in the Grand Ballroom."

"Oh, yes, please!" the girls said eagerly.

Bertram ushered the girls onto the end of the rainbow and Flora flew to join them. Then they were whisked off to Fairyland in a whirl of rainbow colours.

When they arrived at the Fairyland palace, Kirsty and Rachel were thrilled to see everyone waiting for them. The Grand Ballroom had been decorated with glittering white and pink decorations, and all the fairies were in wonderful costumes.

"Welcome!" said King Oberon.
He was dressed as King Arthur, and
Queen Titania was by his side, dressed
as Lady Guinevere.

"We want to thank you for making
sure all Flora's magic items are where
they belong," the Queen told them.

"That means *our* party will be a success as well as Lindsay's. And Jack Frost and his goblins are coming, too. We sent them an invitation they couldn't refuse!"

Before Rachel and Kirsty could reply, a magic rainbow streamed in through an open window, depositing a scowling Jack Frost on the floor.

A moment later, another rainbow whooshed through the same window, and all the goblins tumbled off the end of it as if they were falling out of a chute. Grumbling, they picked themselves up.

"You must be in costume to attend our party, Jack Frost," King Oberon said firmly. "Flora's magic will give you any fancy dress outfit you like. Now, what will it be?"

Rachel and Kirsty watched as Jack Frost frowned in thought.

"I want to be a pirate king!" he declared at last.

Flora fluttered over to him and waved her wand over his head. Sparkling fairy dust instantly transformed Jack Frost into a pirate king, complete with an eye-patch, gold hoop earring and big black boots. He was also wearing an extremely large pirate hat.

Rachel and Kirsty grinned to see that the goblins were now wearing pirate costumes too. Some of them even had peg legs, and parrots on their shoulders.

Looking very pleased with himself, Jack Frost strode off towards the tables laden with party food. "Come along, me hearties!" he shouted in a piratical way.

"Aye-aye, Captain!" the goblins yelled. And they followed Jack Frost, waving their cutlasses enthusiastically.

"Don't worry," Flora told the girls, "the swords aren't sharp at all." She looked down at her mermaid costume. "It's a new party, so I need a new outfit!" she remarked.

Rachel and Kirsty watched as Flora waved her wand above her head. Purple and black sparkles surrounded her for a moment, and her mermaid tail changed to a black frilly dress.

A large black pointed hat appeared on her head, and suddenly she was hovering in the air on a broomstick.

"You're a witch!" Kirsty cried.

"A very friendly-looking witch," Rachel pointed out. And then she and Kirsty laughed as a tiny black cat appeared at the end of the broomstick, mewing loudly.

Flora grinned at them and flew down from her broomstick. The broom and the cat immediately followed her.

"Girls, thank you for coming," said
Queen Titania, "but it's time for you to
return to McKersey Castle."

Rachel and Kirsty gave Flora a big
hug. Then all the fairies gathered round

in their wonderful costumes to wave to the girls as the Queen raised her wand.

"Goodbye!" called Rachel and Kirsty as they were whisked away on a cloud of fairy magic.

Almost instantly, Rachel and Kirsty found themselves outside the ballroom at McKersey Castle. They could hear music playing inside, and people talking and laughing.

"It sounds like the party's going well," Rachel remarked, pushing open the doors as the girls walked through.

But Kirsty wasn't listening. She was

staring down at the harps on the table.

"Rachel," she said softly, in a thrilled voice, "our harps aren't cardboard any more. The fairies must have made them *real*!"

She ran her fingers over the silver strings and four clear, melodic notes rang out.

Rachel smiled dreamily at her own harp. "Isn't fairy magic *wonderful*?" she said, peeping into the ballroom where people were dancing beneath the glittering chandeliers. "Fairy magic is the best!" Kirsty agreed happily, and the girls went into the ballroom to join the party.

Win a Rainbow Magic
Sparkly T-Shirt and Goody Bag!

There are seven magic masks in Flora the Fancy Dress
Fairy and each one has a secret letter in it. Find all
seven letters and re-arrange them to make
a special word, then send it to us.
Each month we will put the entries into a draw.
The winner will receive a Rainbow Magic
Sparkly T-shirt and Goody Bag!

Send your entry on a postcard to: Rainbow Magic
Flora Competition, Orchard Books,
338 Euston Road, London NW1 3BH.
Australian readers should write to
Level 17/207 Kent Street, Sydney, NSW 2000.
New Zealand readers should write to
Rainbow Magic Competition, 4 Whetu Place,
Mairangi Bay, Auckland, NZ.
Don't forget to include your name and address.
Only one entry per child.
Final draw: 30th May 2008

RUBY THE RED FAIRY
978-1-84362-016-7

AMBER THE ORANGE FAIRY
978-1-84362-017-4

SAFFRON THE YELLOW FAIRY
978-1-84362-018-1

FERN THE GREEN FAIRY
978-1-84362-019-8

SKY THE BLUE FAIRY
978-1-84362-020-4

IZZY THE INDIGO FAIRY
978-1-84362-021-1

HEATHER THE VIOLET FAIRY
978-1-84362-022-8

The Weather Fairies

GOLDIE THE SUNSHINE FAIRY
978-1-84362-641-1

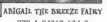

PEARL THE CLOUD FAIRY
978-1-84362-635-0

ABIGAIL THE BREEZE FAIRY
978-1-84362-634-3

CRYSTAL THE SNOW FAIRY
978-1-84362-633-6

HAYLEY THE RAIN FAIRY
978-1-84362-638-1

STORM THE LIGHTNING FAIRY
978-1-84362-637-4

EVIE THE MIST FAIRY
978-1-84362-636-7

The Party Fairies

HONEY THE SWEET FAIRY
978-1-84362-821-7

GRACE THE GLITTER FAIRY
978-1-84362-820-0

MELODIE THE MUSIC FAIRY
978-1-84362-819-4

CHERRY THE CAKE FAIRY
978-1-84362-818-7

JASMINE THE PRESENT FAIRY
978-1-84362-824-8

PHOEBE THE FASHION FAIRY
978-1-84362-823-1

POLLY THE PARTY FUN FAIRY
978-1-84362-822-4

RAINBOW magic ®

The Jewel Fairies

CHLOE THE TOPAZ FAIRY
978-1-84362-956-6

EMILY THE EMERALD FAIRY
978-1-84362-955-9

SCARLETT THE GARNET FAIRY   978-1-84362-954-2

INDIA THE MOONSTONE FAIRY   978-1-84362-958-0

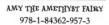

LUCY THE DIAMOND FAIRY
978-1-84362-959-7

SOPHIE THE SAPPHIRE FAIRY
978-1-84362-953-5

AMY THE AMETHYST FAIRY
978-1-84362-957-3

RAINBOW magic ®

The Pet Keeper Fairies

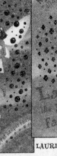

LAUREN THE PUPPY FAIRY
978-1-84616-169-8

GEORGIA THE GUINEA PIG FAIRY
978-1-84616-168-1

BELLA THE BUNNY FAIRY
978-1-84616-170-4

KATIE THE KITTEN FAIRY
978-1-84616-166-7

PENNY THE PONY FAIRY
978-1-84616-171-1

MOLLY THE GOLDFISH FAIRY
978-1-84616-172-8

HARRIET THE HAMSTER FAIRY
978-1-84616-167-4

The Fun Day Fairies

THEA THE THURSDAY FAIRY
978-1-84616-191-9

WILLOW THE WEDNESDAY FAIRY   978-1-84616-190-2

TALLULAH THE TUESDAY FAIRY   978-1-84616-189-6

MEGAN THE MONDAY FAIRY
978-1-84616-188-9

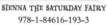

SARAH THE SUNDAY FAIRY
978-1-84616-194-0

SIENNA THE SATURDAY FAIRY   978-1-84616-193-3

FREYA THE FRIDAY FAIRY
978-1-84616-192-6

RAINBOW magic

The Petal Fairies

TIA THE TULIP FAIRY
978-1-84616-457-6

PIPPA THE POPPY FAIRY
978-1-84616-458-3

LOUISE THE LILY FAIRY
978-1-84616-459-0

CHARLOTTE THE
SUNFLOWER FAIRY
978-1-84616-460-6

OLIVIA THE ORCHID FAIRY
978-1-84616-461-3

DANIELLE THE DAISY FAIRY
978-1-84616-462-0

ELLA THE ROSE FAIRY
978-1-84616-464-4

Look out for the Dance Fairies!

BETHANY
THE BALLET FAIRY
978-1-84616-490-3

JADE
THE DISCO FAIRY
978-1-84616-491-0

REBECCA
THE ROCK 'N' ROLL FAIRY
978-1-84616-492-7

TASHA
THE TAP DANCE FAIRY
978-1-84616-493-4

JESSICA
THE JAZZ FAIRY
978-1-84616-495-8

SASKIA
THE SALSA FAIRY
978-1-84616-496-5

IMOGEN
THE ICE DANCE FAIRY
978-1-84616-497-2

HOLLY THE CHRISTMAS FAIRY

978-1-84362-661-9

SUMMER THE HOLIDAY FAIRY

978-1-84362-960-3

STELLA THE STAR FAIRY

978-1-84362-869-9

KYLIE THE CARNIVAL FAIRY

978-1-84616-175-9

PAIGE THE PANTOMIME FAIRY
978-1-84616-209-1

THE RAINBOW MAGIC TREASURY
978-1-84616-047-9

FASHION FAIRY DRESS-UP BOOK
978-1-84616-047-9

FAIRY FRIENDS STICKER BOOK
978-1-84616-209-1

The books in each series are priced at £3.99. *Holly the Christmas Fairy,
Summer the Holiday Fairy, Stella the Star Fairy, Kylie the Carnival Fairy*
and *Paige the Pantomime Fairy* are priced at £5.99.
Fashion Fairy Dress-Up Book and *Fairy Friends Sticker Book* are priced at £3.99.
The Rainbow Magic Treasury is priced at £12.99.
Rainbow Magic books are available from all good bookshops, or can be ordered
direct from the publisher: Orchard Books, PO BOX 29, Douglas IM99 1BQ
Credit card orders please telephone 01624 836000
or fax 01624 837033 or visit our Internet site: www.wattspub.co.uk
or e-mail: bookshop@enterprise.net for details.

To order please quote title, author and ISBN and your full name and address.
Cheques and postal orders should be made payable to 'Bookpost plc.'
Postage and packing is FREE within the UK
(overseas customers should add £2.00 per book).
Prices and availability are subject to change.

Have you checked out the

website at:

www.rainbowmagic.co.uk

There are games, activities and fun things to do, as well as news and information about Rainbow Magic and all of the fairies.